Jake Baked the Cake

By B.G. HENNESSY
Pictures by MARY MORGAN

VIKING

VIKING
Published by the Penguin Group
Viking Penguin, a division of Penguin Books USA Inc.,
40 West 23rd Street, New York, New York 10010, U.S.A.
Penguin Books Ltd, 27 Wrights Lane, London W8 5TZ, England
Penguin Books Australia Ltd, Ringwood, Victoria, Australia
Penguin Books Canada Ltd, 2801 John Street, Markham, Ontario, Canada L3R 1B4
Penguin Books (N.Z.) Ltd, 182–190 Wairau Road, Auckland 10, New Zealand

Penguin Books Ltd, Registered Offices: Harmondsworth, Middlesex, England

First published in 1990 by Viking Penguin, a division of Penguin Books USA Inc.
1   3   5   7   9   10   8   6   4   2
Text copyright © B.G. Hennessy, 1990
Illustrations copyright © Mary Morgan, 1990
All rights reserved

LIBRARY OF CONGRESS CATALOGING-IN-PUBLICATION DATA
Hennessy, B.G. (Barbara G.) Jake baked the cake
B.G. Hennessy ; pictures by Mary Morgan. p.   cm.
Summary: To prepare for the wedding, Sally Price buys the rice, the best man
hires a band, Mr. Fine paints a sign, and Jake bakes a magnificent cake.
ISBN 0-670-82237-X
[1. Weddings—Fiction.   2. Cakes—Fiction.   3. Stories in rhyme.]
I. Morgan, Mary, ill.   II. Title.
PZ8.3.H418Jak   1990   [E]—dc20   89-8948

Printed in Japan.
Set in Goudy Old Style.

For Jim
B.G.H.

The bride's gown was made in town,

The groom's pants arrived from France,

The champagne came from Spain,

While Jake baked the cake.

Sally Price bought the rice,

The best man hired a band,

Mr. Fine painted the sign,

While Jake baked the cake.

Aunt Kris stacked up the gifts,

The flower girls got some curls,

The little boys made lots of noise,

While Jake baked the cake.

The bridesmaids' roses tickled their noses,

The ushers' ties were all the wrong size,

The groom forgot to bring the ring,

While Jake baked the cake.

The guests arrived to see the bride,

Preacher Gray led the way,

Mrs. King began to sing,

While Jake baked the cake.

The mothers cried,

The guests sighed,

The father gave away the bride,

While Jake baked the cake.

The Preacher asked, "Will you?"

The groom vowed, "I do."

The bride said, "Me too!"

And then they all ate the cake,

The pride and joy of baker Jake.